MOLLY'S PUPPY TALE

MOLLY · 1944

BY VALERIE TRIPP

ILLUSTRATIONS NICK BACKES

VIGNETTES NICK BACKES, SUSAN MCALILEY,

KEITH SKEEN

THE AMERICAN GIRLS COLLECTION®

Published by Pleasant Company Publications
Previously published in *American Girl*® magazine
Copyright © 2003 by Pleasant Company
For information, address: Book Editor, Pleasant Company Publications,
8400 Fairway Place, P.O. Box 620998, Middleton, WI 53562.

Visit our Web site at **americangirl.com**

Printed in Singapore.
03 04 05 06 07 08 09 10 TWP 10 9 8 7 6 5 4 3
Library of Congress Cataloging-in-Publication Data

Tripp, Valerie, 1951–
Molly's puppy tale / by Valerie Tripp ; illustrations, Nick Backes ;
vignettes, Nick Backes, Susan McAliley, Keith Skeen.
p. cm. — (The American girls collection)
Summary: In 1945, ten-year-old Molly does not want to share her puppy Bennett
with her brother but finds she might need to change her mind.

ISBN 1-58485-695-5
[1. Dogs—Fiction. 2. Pets—Fiction. 3. Jealousy—Fiction. 4. Brothers and sisters—
Fiction.] I. Backes, Nick, ill. II. McAliley, Susan, ill. III. Title. IV. Series.
PZ7.T7363 Motf 2003   [Fic]—dc21   2002031290

The
AMERICAN GIRLS
COLLECTION®

OTHER AMERICAN GIRLS
SHORT STORIES:

KAYA AND THE RIVER GIRL

THANKS TO JOSEFINA

KIRSTEN'S PROMISE

ADDY'S SUMMER PLACE

SAMANTHA'S SPECIAL TALENT

KIT'S TREE HOUSE

PICTURE CREDITS

The following individuals and organizations have generously given permission to reprint illustrations contained in "Looking Back": p. 30—© David Young-Wolff/PhotoEdit/PictureQuest; p. 31— Lassie® is a registered trademark of Golden Books Publishing Company, Inc. All rights reserved. *On Leave*, Printed by permission of the Norman Rockwell Family Agency, copyright © 1945 the Norman Rockwell Family Entities; p. 33—National Geographic Image Collection (ID 495667); p. 34—Copyright © 1946 Charles Scribner's Sons, New York; p. 35—Reproduced from *Dogs of War*, by John Behan, copyright © 1946 Charles Scribner's Sons, New York; p. 36—Sentry dog, U.S. Coast Guard Photography, courtesy of USCG Historian's Office; p. 37—Messenger dog, National Geographic Image Collection (ID 744625), photo by J. Baylor Roberts; p. 38—Bettmann/CORBIS; p. 39—Copyright © 1946 Charles Scribner's Sons, New York; p. 40—Bettmann/CORBIS; p. 41—Quartermaster Museum, Fort Lee, VA; p. 42—Photography by Jamie Young. Waffle recipe from *Three Dog Bakery™ Cookbook* by Dan Dye and Mark Beckloff, Andrews McMeel Publishing.

TABLE OF CONTENTS

MOLLY'S FAMILY

DAD
*Molly's father, a doctor
who is somewhere in
England, taking care of
wounded soldiers.*

MOM
*Molly's mother, who
holds the family together
while Dad is away.*

MOLLY
*A ten-year-old who
is growing up on
the home front
in America during
World War Two.*

JILL
*Molly's fourteen-year-old
sister, who is always trying
to act grown-up.*

RICKY
*Molly's twelve-year-old
brother—a big pest.*

BRAD
*Molly's five-year-old
brother—a little pest.*

LINDA
*One of Molly's best friends,
a practical schemer.*

SUSAN
*Molly's other best friend,
a cheerful dreamer.*

MRS. GILFORD
*The housekeeper, who
rules the roost when
Mom is at work.*

MOLLY'S
PUPPY TALE

Molly McIntire and her two best friends, Linda and Susan, were hurrying to Molly's house after school on a sunny afternoon in May. They couldn't wait to play with Molly's puppy, Bennett.

"You are so lucky, Molly," sighed Susan. "I wish I had a dog of my very own, especially one like Bennett. He's *adorable*."

"He's smart, too," said Linda. "He'll be like Lassie, probably, when he grows up."

Molly smiled. She believed Linda and

1

Susan were absolutely right. Bennett was the cutest and smartest puppy in the world. She loved everything about him, from his soft black nose to his always wagging tail. He was lively and cuddly and full of affection. "Bennett already knows his name," Molly told her friends. "This morning he ran straight to me when I called him."

"Gosh!" said Susan. "That *is* smart for a puppy. You've only had him since your birthday in April."

"Most nights I put his basket right on the bed next to me so he won't feel lonely," said Molly.

"Oh, that's so sweet!" said Susan.

"Do you ever get tired of taking care of

him?" asked Linda, who liked to ask practical questions.

"Oh, no," said Molly. "I'd do anything for Bennett. I love him. And he loves me best of anyone in the world."

When the girls got to Molly's house, they said hello to Mrs. Gilford, the McIntires' housekeeper. She was working in her Victory garden, turning over the earth to get it ready for spring planting. Ricky was outside, too, playing tug-of-war with Bennett. Ricky was holding on to one end of an old rag, and Bennett's jaws were clamped onto the other end. Bennett was tossing his head, growling,

3

and wagging his tail wildly.

Molly hardly recognized the muddy, frisky dog as her sweet, cuddly puppy. She felt a little pinch of annoyance. Bennett was clearly having a great time—without her.

"Bennett!" she called. "Here, boy! Come here, Bennett!"

Bennett did not even glance her way.

Molly clapped her hands and whistled. "Bennett! Come!" she called, a little louder this time. "Come here now!"

Bennett ignored her.

Now Molly was more than annoyed. She had just bragged to Linda and Susan about how much Bennett loved her, and now Ricky was making it look as if Bennett liked *him* better than he liked *her!*

Ricky didn't notice the frown on Molly's face. "Hey, look at this!" he said. "I taught Bennett how to fetch a ball." He tossed the ball past Molly. "Go get it, boy!" he said to Bennett.

Bennett bounded after the ball. But before he got to it, Molly snatched him up in her arms. "Just look at him," she said to Ricky crossly. "You've gotten him all muddy."

"And you tired him out," Susan accused.

"And he was having so much fun with you, he didn't pay attention when Molly called him," added Linda, pointing out the exact thing Molly had hoped no one else had noticed.

5

"A little mud won't hurt him," said Ricky. "Bennett's not a baby anymore. He wants to rough-and-tumble with me. He likes it. And it's good for him."

"*I'll* decide what's good for him," said Molly sharply. "He's *my* puppy." Bennett squirmed in her arms, trying to get down. Molly tightened her grip, turned her back on Ricky, and marched into the house. Linda and Susan followed her, leaving behind whatever else Ricky had to say.

★

That night, Molly put Bennett's basket right next to her pillow. Bennett licked her face with his rough tongue,

then nestled down and fell asleep. Molly fell asleep, too, with her hand on his warm little head.

In the middle of the night, Molly woke up. She peeked into the basket to be sure Bennett was sleeping peacefully.

Bennett was gone.

Molly sat up, switched on her lamp, and put on her glasses. "Bennett?" she said anxiously. "Bennett?" Quickly, she looked under the beds, behind the chair, under her dressing table, and even in the closet. Bennett was nowhere to be found.

"Bennett!" Molly whispered. "Where *are* you?"

Molly tiptoed out into the hall. Ricky's door was open, so she peered into his room. There was Bennett, curled up at the foot of Ricky's bed, his sweet, sleeping face resting on his paws.

Molly's heart sank. Could it be that Bennett really *was* beginning to like Ricky more than he liked her? Right then and there, she made up her mind that she would not share Bennett with Ricky at all anymore. She scooped the puppy up off Ricky's bed, carried him back to her room, and put him in his basket. She was careful to close her bedroom door so that it was shut tight.

★

The next morning, Molly came down late to breakfast. She felt cranky and out of

*There was Bennett, curled up at the foot of Ricky's bed,
his sweet, sleeping face resting on his paws.*

sorts as she let Bennett out the back door.

"You're too late for pancakes," said Mrs. Gilford. She was at the sink, watering seedlings she'd nursed along through the winter for her Victory garden. "It'll have to be cornflakes. Get yourself a bowl."

Ricky jumped up from the table. "I'll feed Bennett," he said.

"No, you will *not*," said Molly.

"What's eating you?" asked Ricky. "I'm just trying to do you a favor."

"Well, I don't need any favors from you," said Molly as she poured too much milk on her cornflakes. "I can take care of Bennett all by myself. You will not do *anything* with him *anymore*. That's final."

An unhappy look crossed Ricky's face. Then he shrugged. "Fine with me, Miss Selfish," he said. He grabbed his schoolbooks and slammed out the door.

Molly ate her soggy cornflakes in silence. When she went to the sink to rinse out her bowl and fix Bennett's breakfast, Mrs. Gilford spoke to her.

"If you ask me, that dog is being mollycoddled. He's not a helpless little ball of fur anymore," she said. "Soon he'll reach the chewing stage, and nothing will be safe. Mark my words, you'll have to keep your eye on him every minute. And he's going to need exercise and training, too. If you're smart, you'll let your brother Ricky help you."

"I don't need his help!" Molly said. "Bennett is my dog, and I will be responsible for him."

Mrs. Gilford raised her eyebrows. "Very well," she said. "But remember, you might be able to keep Bennett out of trouble, but there's no way you can keep him from liking other people. You can pen up a dog, but you can't pen up his affections. It isn't right, and anyway, it's impossible."

Molly did not want to hear any more. She put Bennett in his pen, fed him, kissed him, and hurried off to school.

★

For the next week or so, Molly had no
trouble taking care of Bennett all by her-
self. He seemed happy to spend the day in
his pen snoozing. Molly played with him
when she came home from school, and he
usually fell asleep at her feet while she
was doing her homework in her room
after dinner.

But as time passed, taking care of
Bennett became more of a problem. One
day, Molly stayed after school for Girl
Scouts and came home later than usual.
Bennett went crazy barking as soon as he
saw her. He scrabbled wildly with his
paws in the dirt. When Molly opened his
pen, he bolted past her! He scooted under

the hedge and ran off down the block.

"Bennett!" Molly yelled as she chased after him. "Bennett! Come back!"

But Bennett seemed to think it was great fun to have Molly chasing him and shouting at him. Molly couldn't grab hold of him until he stopped to scatter the neighbors' newspaper all over their lawn.

"Now why'd you run off like that?" Molly asked Bennett as she carried him home. "I guess you were tired of being in your pen." Molly knew the puppy had never been left alone for such a long time before. Ricky used to play with him on Girl Scout days. Molly realized that from now on, she'd have to come straight home from school to care for Bennett.

And that's exactly what Molly did.
But even so, the next few
weeks were difficult. If Molly
took her eyes off Bennett for one
second, he got into mischief.
He tracked mud across the
kitchen floor that Mrs. Gilford
had just washed. He grabbed
Linda's bag lunch and ate it in
one gulp. He chewed up a letter
from Dad that Mom had not even
read yet.

Molly had to admit that Ricky
and Mrs. Gilford had been right
about one thing. Now that Bennett
was older, he *was* a lot friskier. It was
no longer enough just to cuddle and

15

baby him. Molly realized that he needed to be more active. So she began to throw sticks for Bennett to fetch. She played tug-of-war with Bennett and took him for long walks on his leash. Bennett loved his walks. He sniffed enthusiastically at every tree, bush, and pole and barked a friendly hello to every person they passed.

Of course, all of this new exercise took up most of Molly's free time. Some days she felt as if *she* were the one on a leash. But Molly was determined not to share her dog. She was still convinced that she could do everything for Bennett. He did not need anyone else but her.

★

As Molly and Bennett set forth on their walk one day, Bennett stopped suddenly. He barked eagerly and wagged his tail hard.

"What is it, Bennett?" Molly asked. Then she saw. It was Ricky. He was in the driveway shooting baskets. Bennett strained at the leash, trying to get to him.

"No, Bennett," said Molly quickly. She tried to drag him away for their walk, but he refused to go. Finally, Molly picked him up. He squirmed in her arms, whining and wiggling, struggling to get down.

Molly decided to bring him up to her room and play with him there. She felt a

17

little guilty because no matter what she did to amuse him, he kept scratching at the door, begging to go out. He didn't give up until the sound of the basketball bouncing on the driveway had stopped.

By then, Bennett had worn himself out. Molly left him asleep in his basket when she went to dinner. When she came back upstairs to do her homework, she could not believe her eyes.

"Oh, Bennett!" she gasped. It looked as if it had snowed in her room. Bennett had ripped open her pillow and scattered the feathers everywhere! He had eaten several chapters of her arithmetic work-book, chewed the sleeve off her best blouse, and gnawed on the handle of her book bag.

Worst of all, he had ripped the heads off her precious princess paper dolls.

"Bennett, you are a very bad dog!" scolded Molly. Bennett just looked up at her with his big soft eyes. Molly grimly set to work cleaning up the mess.

★

After school a few days later, Linda asked, "Want to come over to my house and jump rope with Susan and me?"

Molly hesitated. She knew Bennett was waiting for her. But it was such a beautiful spring day! And it had been so long since she had had an afternoon off from dog duty. Surely Bennett couldn't do any harm while he was safely in his pen.

"Well, I guess it would be O.K. for just a little while," she said at last.

Jumping rope was fun, and Molly stayed longer than she'd meant to. When she got home, Bennett met her at the end of the driveway, grinning a slobbery doggy grin and looking very pleased with himself.

"How did you get out of your pen?" Molly asked him. She sighed with exasperation when she saw that Bennett had dug an enormous hole and had made himself an escape tunnel out of his pen.

"Bad dog!" Molly said sternly. "You shouldn't have dug like that!"

Bennett didn't look the least bit sorry. He barked happily and scampered off to play.

While Molly was kicking the dirt back into the hole Bennett had dug, she happened to look over at Mrs. Gilford's Victory garden. Her jaw dropped. She walked toward the garden, staring in dismay.

The seedlings Mrs. Gilford had tended so long and transplanted so lovingly had been yanked out of the ground. Bulbs were dug up and gnawed. The seed-packet labels that used to stand so proudly at the end of every row were torn and scattered. Even the rocks Mrs. Gilford had lined up around the edges of the garden had been knocked every which way. All of Mrs. Gilford's careful work was ruined. It had been torn apart by the paws and jaws of Bennett.

Molly knelt, defeated and miserable, in the dirt at the edge of what used to be the Victory garden.

"Looks pretty bad," said Ricky. He was standing behind her.

*Molly knelt, defeated and miserable, in the dirt
at the edge of what used to be the Victory garden.*

"Yeah," said Molly.

"Mrs. Gilford's going to be mad," said Ricky.

"Yeah," said Molly again.

"You know," Ricky went on, "today is Friday. Mrs. Gilford won't be back until Monday morning. We could clean up this mess and get a good start at replanting everything by Monday if we worked at it this weekend."

"You'd help me?" Molly asked. She couldn't believe her ears.

"Yeah, well, you'd have to pay me back somehow," said Ricky.

"How?" asked Molly. She was suspicious, but she was desperate, too.

"Bennett," said Ricky quickly. "Let me

play with him and teach him stuff and help take care of him."

Molly didn't answer. Just then, Bennett ran to her with something in his mouth. He stood in front of her wagging his tail so hard, his whole rear end was moving. He nudged her with his head and wriggled with joy when she hugged him. *Oh, Bennett*, Molly thought, *I love you so much.* Molly knew Bennett loved her, too. But she realized that sharing Bennett with Ricky was the right thing for the puppy— and for her.

"O.K.," she said to Ricky. "It's a deal."

"Good," said Ricky. He sat next to Molly and said to Bennett, "Here, boy!"

Bennett jumped up on Ricky, smearing

dirt all over his shirt. Then he jumped on
Molly and dropped what he had in his
mouth so that he could lick her face.

Molly looked down at her lap and saw
one of Mrs. Gilford's gardening gloves.
Bennett had chewed off all the fingers.
Molly grinned. She held the glove up to

show Ricky and said, "You can start sharing Bennett right now. I think he's been mollycoddled long enough!"

VALERIE TRIPP

Sunday at 10 weeks   Now

Valerie Tripp and her family named their dog Sunday because that's the day they first met him. Just like Bennett, Sunday is lively, friendly, and lovable. He also likes to chew things, just as Bennett did. So far, Sunday has chewed up five welcome mats!

Valerie Tripp has written forty-seven books in The American Girls Collection, including eleven about Molly.

LOOKING BACK 1944

A PEEK INTO THE PAST

DOGS IN 1944

During World War Two, dogs played an important role in the war effort—both at home and overseas. On the home front, dogs were loving, lively companions who kept their owners' spirits up. Girls and boys who were responsible for caring for a pet—especially a mischievous puppy like Bennett—had less time to worry about the war.

Even children without pets found comfort in America's favorite furry movie star, Lassie. In the

1943 movie *Lassie Come Home*, the collie is separated from the people she loves and will stop at nothing to find her way back to them. Many children during World War Two knew just how Lassie felt. They, too, were separated from family members—those fighting the war overseas. Perhaps Lassie gave children hope that their loved ones would soon find their way home.

Lassie®

Soldiers and sailors missed their dogs back home.

Some dogs did more than cheer up people on the home front. Between 1942 and 1945, the United States military trained thousands of dogs to work along-side soldiers in the heat of battle. Some worked as guard dogs, others as mes-sengers, and still others as rescue dogs that brought help to wounded soldiers.

Most of the dogs in the military were family pets volunteered by their owners. People with smart, obedient dogs were proud to sign them up for service because it was another way to help the war effort. But not all dogs could become soldiers. Dogs had to weigh at least fifty pounds, be at least twenty inches tall, and be between the ages of one and five. Small dogs like Bennett weren't accepted because it was thought that the enemy wouldn't fear them!

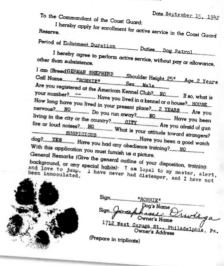

Dogs "signed" their application forms with paw prints.

German shepherds, on the other hand, were natural soldiers. Because of their keen senses, intelligence, and steady nerves, they were the most popular breed in the military. Many other large dogs—from Dobermans to

Dalmatians—joined the service, too.

All dogs that entered the service had to go through basic training. Handlers taught the dogs simple commands like "heel," "sit," "down," "stay," and "come." After basic training, dogs learned more advanced skills, like crawling low to the ground or through barbed wire, climbing up ramps, and jumping over obstacles.

Crawling was usually the first war skill that dogs learned.

The hardest lesson for most dogs, though, was learning not to fear gunfire.

To train dogs, handlers rewarded them with praise and a pat on the head for what

Some dogs even learned to parachute!

was done right—not punishment for what was done wrong. And because dogs learn best from each other, handlers enlisted the help of more experienced dogs when training the new "recruits."

Sentry dogs helped the Coast Guard protect beaches on the home front.

Many dogs were trained to work as *sentry*, or guard, dogs. Because of their sharp senses, dogs were able to warn their handlers if the enemy was nearby. Sentry dogs were especially helpful at night, when most attacks happened. If a sentry dog smelled or heard a stranger approaching, the dog would bark or growl to alert its handler. Other dogs called *scouts* learned to warn their handlers silently so that the enemy wouldn't hear the barking and be able to escape.

Dogs trained as *messengers* carried important information back and forth between two handlers. Maps and letters were placed in metal tubes that were attached to the dogs' collars. If a troop of soldiers was cut off from its command post, the soldiers could send a messenger dog to get help or information about where the enemy was.

A messenger dog receives his mission.

Messenger dogs swam rivers, climbed walls, and crawled through barbed wire—anything to complete their missions. Dogs made good messengers because they could run much faster than men and were lower to the ground, so they were less likely to be seen or shot. Still, many messenger dogs were wounded while on the job. Dick, a black

No wall was too high for this dog to climb!

Labrador retriever, was shot in the back and shoulder while running through enemy territory. He didn't stop running until he had delivered his message. Then, safely back with his handler, Dick died from his wounds.

Human soldiers who were wounded on the battlefield were sometimes helped by another group of military dogs called *rescuers*. Rescue dogs were trained to find wounded soldiers and keep them awake—and alive—until nurses could reach them. And *pack dogs*, which were usually larger

Rescue dogs wore the Red Cross symbol.

*Rescue dogs—with first-aid kits strapped to their backs—
practice leaping over obstacles to get to wounded soldiers.*

breeds like Great Danes and Saint
Bernards, carried medical supplies,
food, and water to soldiers in need.

When the war ended, dogs in the
military were considered true heroes.
These four-footed soldiers had saved
many lives and even may have helped
to shorten the war. But now it was time to

return to their families at home. Military dogs were trained to go back to civilian life, and by 1947, every volunteer dog had been returned to its owner. Imagine how children felt when they were reunited with their pets after so many years!

AN
AMERICAN
GIRLS
PASTIME

MAKE DOG TREATS

Your dog will woof for these waffles!

When dogs in the military performed a task well, they were rewarded with a simple word of praise or a pat on the head. On the home front, though, Molly might have spoiled Bennett with a treat like these waffle-shaped dog biscuits. Even Mrs. Gilford would have approved of this recipe—the biscuits are made without rationed items like meat, sugar, or butter! Try making them for your favorite pooch.

YOU WILL NEED:

🖐 *An adult to help you*

Ingredients

1 teaspoon shortening

4 cups whole wheat flour

½ cup cornmeal

1 egg

2 tablespoons
vegetable oil

1¾ cups water

Equipment

Cookie sheet

Large mixing bowl

Rolling pin

Butter knife

Waffle iron

Plastic storage bags

1. Preheat oven to 325 degrees. Grease the cookie sheet with the shortening.

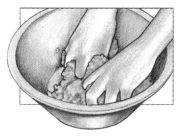

2. Measure remaining ingredients into a large bowl. Use your hands to mix the dough thoroughly.

3. Use the rolling pin to roll out dough until it is ¼ inch thick. Use the knife to cut squares of dough to fit your waffle iron.

4. Press the dough scraps into a ball and repeat step 3 until all dough has been used.

5. Place each square of dough on a cold (unplugged) waffle iron and press.

6. Place "waffles" on a cookie sheet. Have an adult help you bake them for 45 minutes.

7. Let waffles cool. Break them into quarters.

8. Store waffles in plastic storage bags to keep them fresh.

PO BOX 620497
MIDDLETON WI 53562-0497

American Girl ★

Catalogue Request

Join our mailing list! Just drop this card
in the mail, call **1-800-845-0005**, or visit
our Web site at **americangirl.com.**

Send me a catalogue:

Name _____

Address _____

City _____ State ____ Zip 1961i

Girl's birth date: ___ / ___ / ___
         month day year

Send my friend a catalogue:

Name _____

Address _____

City _____ State ____ Zip 1225i

E-mail _____

Parent's signature _____

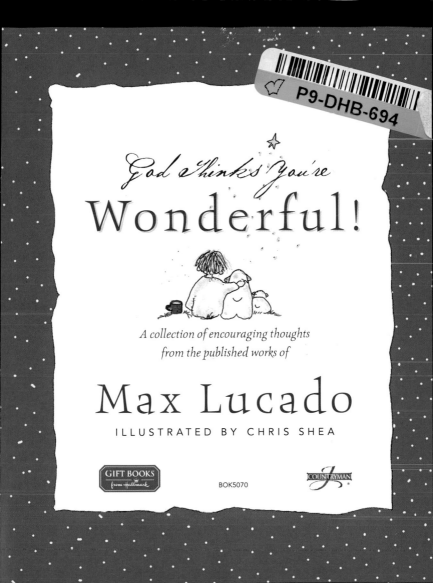

God Thinks You're

Wonderful!

A collection of encouraging thoughts
from the published works of

Max Lucado

ILLUSTRATED BY CHRIS SHEA

GIFT BOOKS
from Hallmark

BOK5070

COUNTRYMAN

For Jack and Marsha Countryman.
God thinks you're wonderful, and so do I.
MAX LUCADO

To my dad, Bill Givens,
with "such happiness."
CHRIS SHEA

God is fond of you . . .

If he had a wallet,

your photo would be in it.

If he had a refrigerator,

your picture would be on it.

He sends you flowers

every spring

and a sunrise

every morning.

good morning

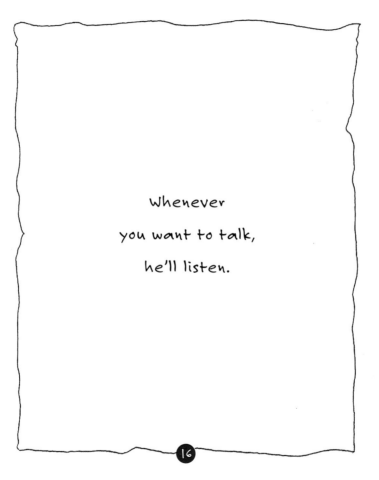

Whenever

you want to talk,

he'll listen.

I'm always listening

He can live anywhere

in the universe,

and he chose

your heart.

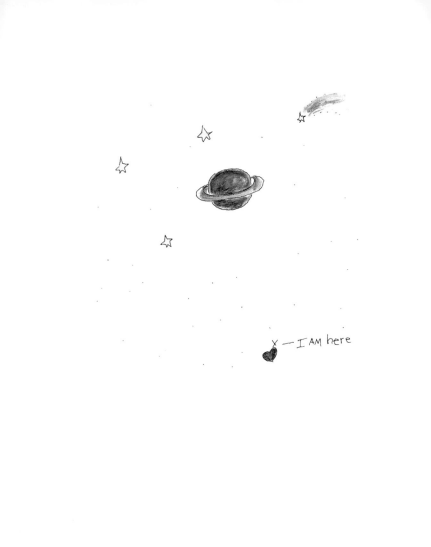

X — I AM here

Face it, friend.

He's crazy about you.

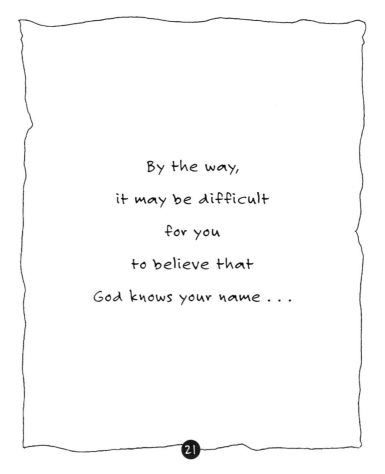

By the way,

it may be difficult

for you

to believe that

God knows your name . . .

but he does.

Written on his hand.

Spoken by his mouth.

whispered by his lips.

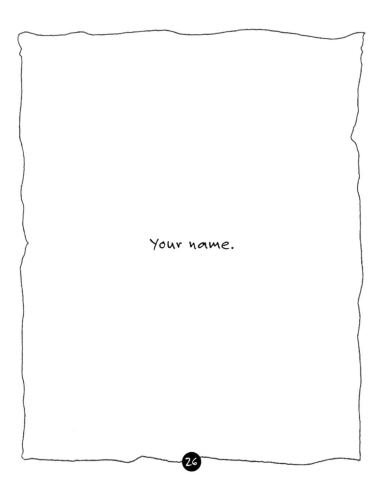

Your name.

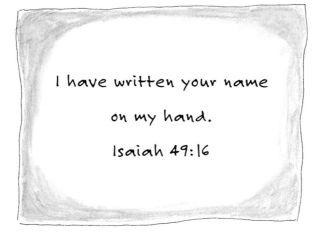

I have written your name

on my hand.

Isaiah 49:16

Blessings
Available

Peace
Love
• Happiness
Parents
Kids
grand Kids
popcicles
Kittens
Sunsets
• carrots
sun
moon
stars

pie
teachers
friends
storms
flowers
• trees
dogs
intelligence
wonder
God
angels
Jesus

Try to
place in →

Our hearts are
not large enough
to contain the blessings
that God wants to give.

So try this.

The next time a sunrise

steals your breath . . .

or a meadow of flowers

leaves you speechless . . .

remain that way.

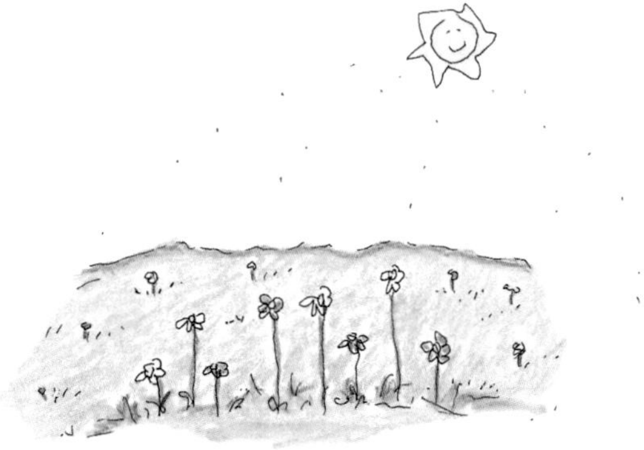

Say nothing and listen

as heaven whispers,

"Do you like it?

I did it just for you."

If we give gifts

to show our love,

how much more

would he?

He could have

left the world

flat and gray . . .

but he didn't.

He splashed orange

in the sunrise . . .

and cast the sky

in blue.

And if you love

to see geese

as they gather,

chances are

you'll see that too.

Did he have to make

the squirrel's tail furry?

Was he obliged

to make the birds sing?

And the funny way

that chickens scurry . . .

or the majesty

of thunder

when it rings?

Why give a flower

fragrance?

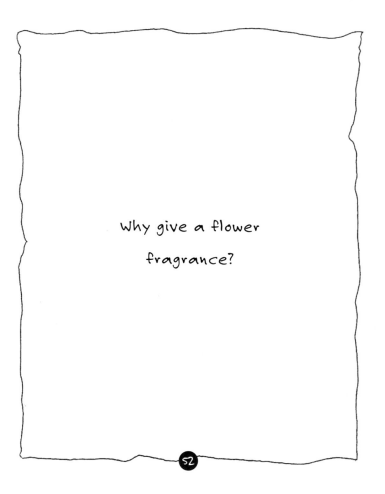

Why give food

its taste?

Could it be

he loves to see

that look

upon your face?

So promise me

you'll never forget . . .

that you aren't

an accident

or an incident . . .

you are a gift

to the world,

a divine work of art,

signed by God.

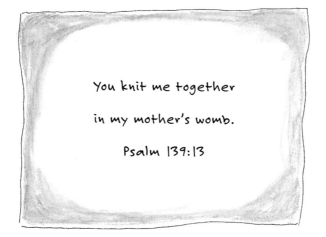

You knit me together

in my mother's womb.

Psalm 139:13

You were

knit together.

63

You weren't

mass-produced.

You aren't an

assembly-line product.

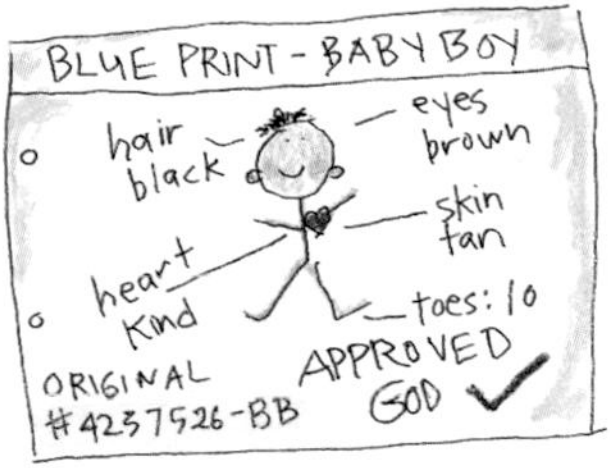
BLUE PRINT - BABY BOY
hair black
eyes brown
skin tan
heart kind
toes: 10
ORIGINAL
#4237526-BB
APPROVED
GOD

You were

deliberately planned,

specifically gifted,

and lovingly positioned

on this earth . . .

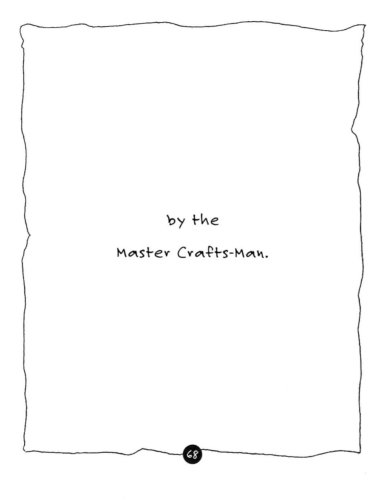

by the

Master Crafts-Man.

68

He thinks you are

the best thing

to come down the pike

in quite a while.

You can do it!

Turn to the sidelines;

that's God cheering

your run.

Look past the finish line;

that's God

applauding your steps.

God is for you.

Had he a calendar,

your birthday

would be circled.

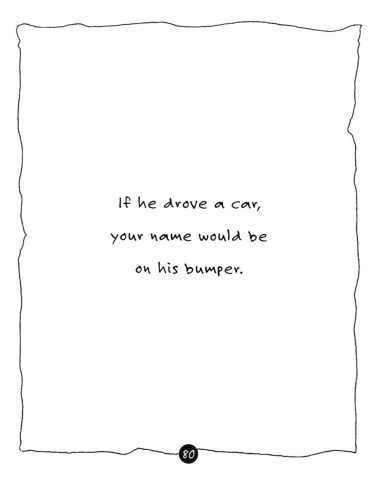

If he drove a car,

your name would be

on his bumper.

If there's a tree in heaven,

he's carved your name

in the bark.

Heaven - 2002

actual un-retouched photo

Maybe you don't want

to trouble God

with your hurts.

But . . .

"he cares about you"

(1 Peter 5:7).

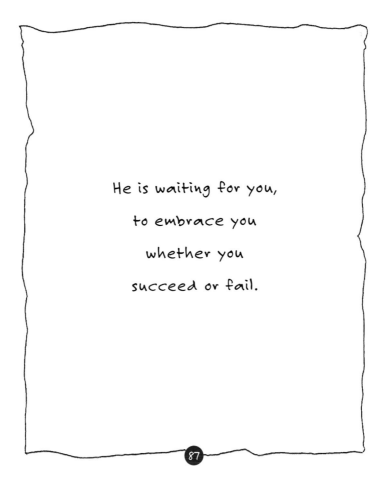

He is waiting for you,

to embrace you

whether you

succeed or fail.

Your heavenly Father is

very fond of you

and only wants to share

his love with you.

MEMO

Blessed be

the LORD your God who

has delighted

in you. . . .

1 Kings 10:9 NKJV

Untethered by time,

God sees us all.

Vagabonds and ragamuffins all, he

saw us before we were born.

And he loves what he sees.

Flooded by emotion,

overcome by pride,

the Starmaker turns to us,

one by one, and says,

"You are my child.

I love you dearly.

I'm aware that

someday you'll turn from me

and walk away.

But I want you to know,

I've already provided

a way back."

You have captured

the heart of God.

He cannot bear to live

without you.

God's dream is

to make you right

with him.

And the path to the cross

tells us exactly how far

God will go to call us back.

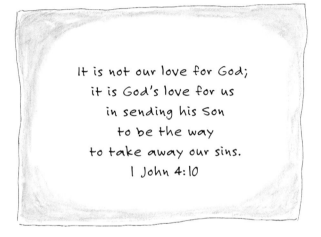

It is not our love for God;
it is God's love for us
in sending his Son
to be the way
to take away our sins.
1 John 4:10

"Can anything make me
stop loving you?" God asks.

"You wonder how long

my love will last?

Watch me speak your language,

sleep on your earth,

and feel your hurts.

Find your answer

on a splintered cross,

on a craggy hill.

That's how much

I love you."

God does more

than forgive our mistakes;

he removes them!

We simply have

to take them to him.

You can talk to God

because God listens.

Let a tear appear
on your cheek, and
he is there to wipe it.

He has sent his angels

to care for you,

his Holy spirit

to dwell in you . . .

his church

to encourage you,

and his word

to guide you.

As much as you want

to see him, he wants

to see you more.

If you want

to touch God's heart,

use the name

he loves to hear.

Call him "Father."

He thinks

you're wonderful!

God Thinks You're

Wonderful!

A collection of encouraging thoughts
from the published works of

Max Lucado

ILLUSTRATED BY CHRIS SHEA

GIFT BOOKS *from Hallmark*

BOK5070

COUNTRYMAN

This edition published under license from J. Countryman®, a trademark of Thomas Nelson, Inc., exclusively for Hallmark Cards, Inc.

Compiled and edited by Terri Gibbs

Editorial Supervision: Karen Hill, Administrative Editor for Max Lucado

www.hallmark.com
www.jcountryman.com

Designed by UDG|DesignWorks, Sisters, Oregon.

ISBN: 1-4041-0074-1

Printed and bound in China

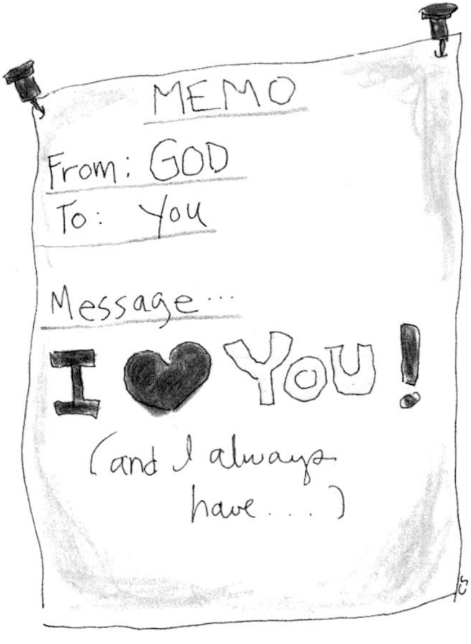
MEMO
From: GOD
To: You
Message...
I ♥ YOU!
(and I always have...)

For Jack and Marsha Countryman.
God thinks you're wonderful, and so do I.
MAX LUCADO

To my dad, Bill Givens,
with "such happiness."
CHRIS SHEA

God is fond of you . . .

If he had a wallet,

your photo would be in it.

If he had a refrigerator,

your picture would be on it.

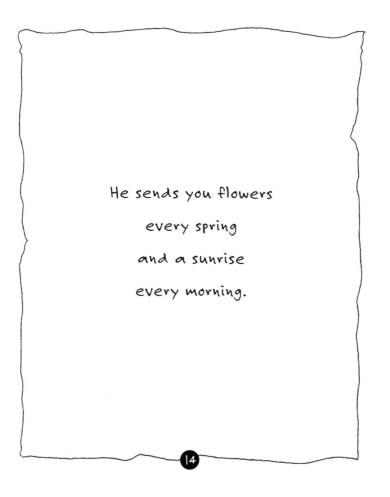

He sends you flowers

every spring

and a sunrise

every morning.

good morning

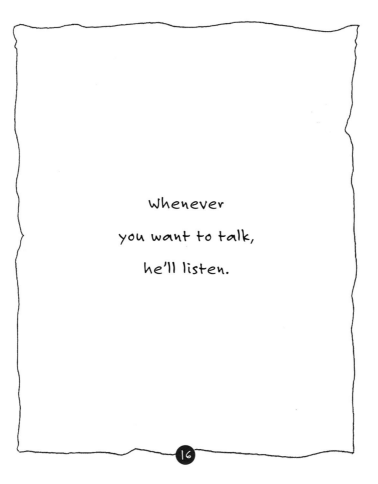

Whenever
you want to talk,
he'll listen.

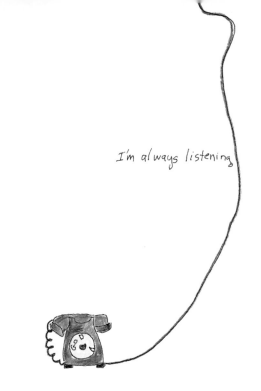

I'm always listening

He can live anywhere

in the universe,

and he chose

your heart.

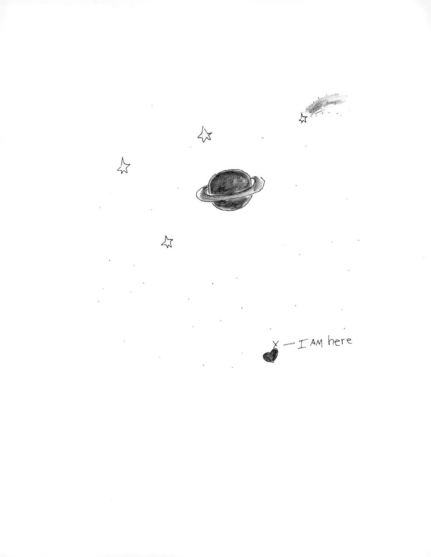

Face it, friend.

He's crazy about you.

By the way,

it may be difficult

for you

to believe that

God knows your name . . .

but he does.

Written on his hand.

Spoken by his mouth.

whispered by his lips.

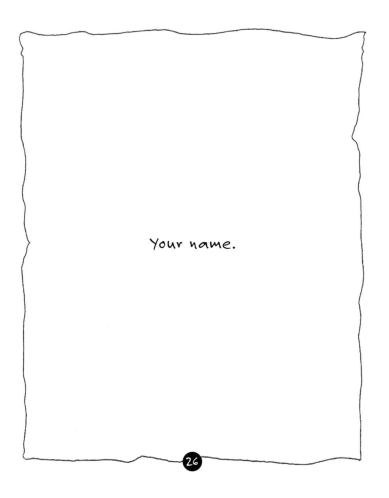

Your name.

26

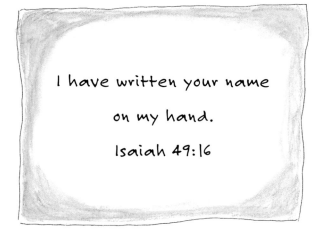

I have written your name

on my hand.

Isaiah 49:16

Blessings
Available

Peace
Love
Happiness
parents
Kids
grand Kids
popcicles
Kittens
Sunsets
carrots
sun
moon
stars
pie
teachers
friends
storms
flowers
trees
dogs
intelligence
wonder
God
angels
Jesus

Try to
place in →

Our hearts are
not large enough
to contain the blessings
that God wants to give.

So try this.

The next time a sunrise

steals your breath . . .

or a meadow of flowers

leaves you speechless . . .

remain that way.

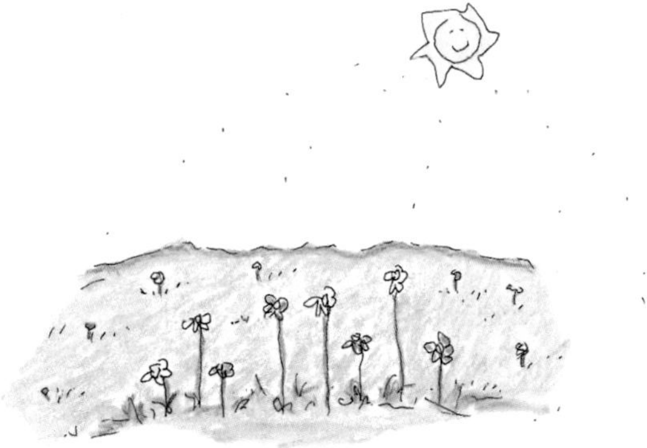

Say nothing and listen

as heaven whispers,

"Do you like it?

I did it just for you."

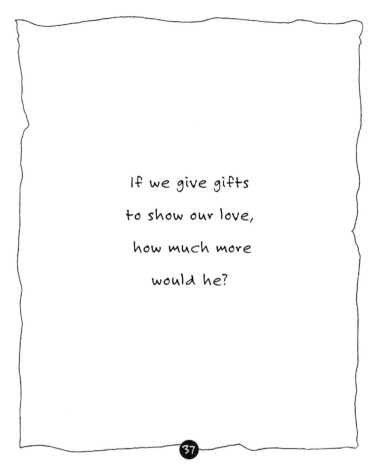

If we give gifts

to show our love,

how much more

would he?

He could have

left the world

flat and gray . . .

but he didn't.

He splashed orange

in the sunrise . . .

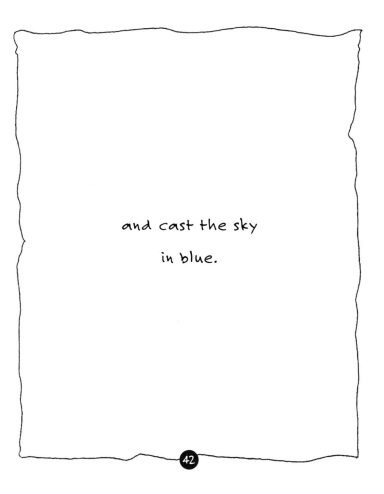

and cast the sky

in blue.

And if you love

to see geese

as they gather,

chances are

you'll see that too.

Did he have to make

the squirrel's tail furry?

was he obliged

to make the birds sing?

And the funny way

that chickens scurry . . .

or the majesty

of thunder

when it rings?

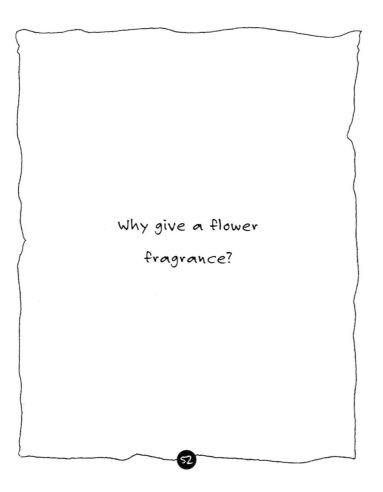

Why give a flower

fragrance?

why give food

its taste?

Could it be

he loves to see

that look

upon your face?

So promise me

you'll never forget . . .

that you aren't

an accident

or an incident . . .

you are a gift

to the world,

a divine work of art,

signed by God.

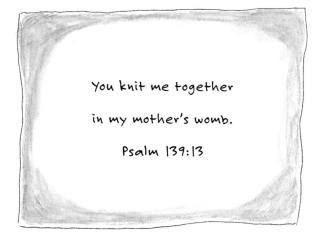

You knit me together

in my mother's womb.

Psalm 139:13

You were

knit together.

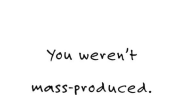

You weren't
mass-produced.
You aren't an
assembly-line product.

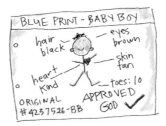

You were

deliberately planned,

specifically gifted,

and lovingly positioned

on this earth . . .

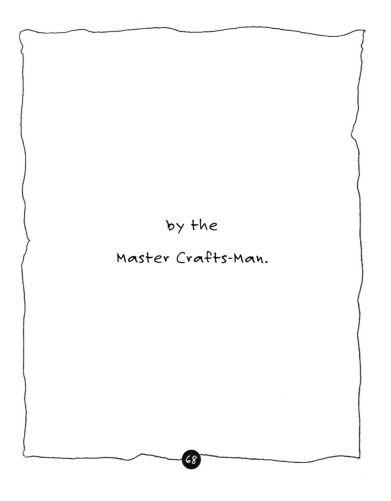

by the

Master Crafts-Man.

Bloom here!

He thinks you are

the best thing

to come down the pike

in quite a while.

You can do it!

Turn to the sidelines;

that's God cheering

your run.

Look past the finish line;

that's God

applauding your steps.

God is for you.

Had he a calendar,

your birthday

would be circled.

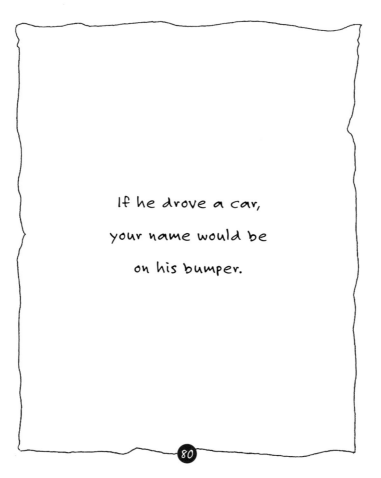

If he drove a car,

your name would be

on his bumper.

If there's a tree in heaven,

he's carved your name

in the bark.

Heaven – 2002

actual un-retouched photo

Maybe you don't want

to trouble God

with your hurts.

But . . .

"he cares about you"

(1 Peter 5:7).

He is waiting for you,

to embrace you

whether you

succeed or fail.

Your heavenly Father is

very fond of you

and only wants to share

his love with you.

MEMO

Blessed be

the LORD your God who

has delighted

in you. . . .

1 Kings 10:9 NKJV

Untethered by time,

God sees us all.

Vagabonds and ragamuffins all, he
saw us before we were born.
And he loves what he sees.

Flooded by emotion,

overcome by pride,

the Starmaker turns to us,

one by one, and says,

"You are my child.

I love you dearly.

I'm aware that

someday you'll turn from me

and walk away.

But I want you to know,

I've already provided

a way back."

You have captured

the heart of God.

He cannot bear to live

without you.

God's dream is

to make you right

with him.

And the path to the cross

tells us exactly how far

God will go to call us back.

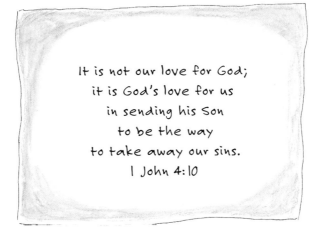

It is not our love for God;
it is God's love for us
in sending his Son
to be the way
to take away our sins.
1 John 4:10

"Can anything make me
stop loving you?" God asks.

"You wonder how long

my love will last?

Watch me speak your language,

sleep on your earth,

and feel your hurts.

Find your answer

on a splintered cross,

on a craggy hill.

That's how much

I love you."

God does more

than forgive our mistakes;

he removes them!

We simply have

to take them to him.

You can talk to God

because God listens.

Let a tear appear

on your cheek, and

he is there to wipe it.

He has sent his angels

to care for you,

his Holy spirit

to dwell in you . . .

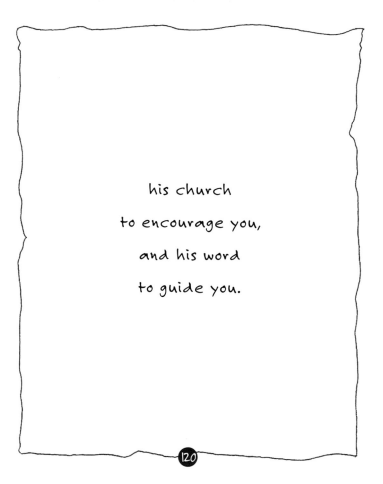

his church

to encourage you,

and his word

to guide you.

As much as you want

to see him, he wants

to see you more.

If you want
to touch God's heart,
use the name
he loves to hear.

Call him "Father."

He thinks

you're wonderful!